Angles
to
Zeros

Mathematics from A to Z

Colleen Dolphin

Consulting Editor, Diane Craig, M.A./Reading Specialist

ABDO
Publishing Company

Published by ABDO Publishing Company, 8000 West 78th Street, Edina, Minnesota 55439. Copyright © 2009 by Abdo Consulting Group, Inc. International copyrights reserved in all countries. No part of this book may be reproduced in any form without written permission from the publisher. Super SandCastle™ is a trademark and logo of ABDO Publishing Company.

Printed in the United States.

Editor: Pam Price
Content Developer: Nancy Tuminelly
Cover and Interior Design and Production: Colleen Dolphin, Mighty Media
Photo Credits: Shutterstock

Library of Congress Cataloging-in-Publication Data

Dolphin, Colleen, 1979-

　Angles to zeros : mathematics from A to Z / Colleen Dolphin.

　　p. cm. -- (Let's look A to Z)

　ISBN 978-1-60453-011-7

　1. Mathematics--Juvenile literature. I. Title.

　QA40.5.D66 2009

　510--dc22

2007050951

Super SandCastle™ books are created by a team of professional educators, reading specialists, and content developers around five essential components—phonemic awareness, phonics, vocabulary, text comprehension, and fluency—to assist young readers as they develop reading skills and strategies and increase their general knowledge. All books are written, reviewed, and leveled for guided reading, early reading intervention, and Accelerated Reader® programs for use in shared, guided, and independent reading and writing activities to support a balanced approach to literacy instruction.

About Super SandCastle™

Bigger Books for Emerging Readers
Grades K-4

Created for library, classroom, and at-home use, Super SandCastle™ books support and engage young readers as they develop and build literacy skills and will increase their general knowledge about the world around them. Super SandCastle™ books are part of SandCastle™, the leading preK–3 imprint for emerging and beginning readers. Super SandCastle™ features a larger trim size for more reading fun.

Let Us Know

Super SandCastle™ would like to hear your stories about reading this book. What was your favorite page? Was there something hard that you needed help with? Share the ups and downs of learning to read. We want to hear from you! Send us an e-mail.

sandcastle@abdopublishing.com

Contact us for a complete list of SandCastle™, Super SandCastle™, and other nonfiction and fiction titles from ABDO Publishing Company.

www.abdopublishing.com • 8000 West 78th Street Edina, MN 55439 • 800-800-1312 • 952-831-1632 fax

This fun and informative series employs illustrated definitions to introduce emerging readers to an alphabet of words in various topic areas. Each page combines words with corresponding images and descriptive sentences to encourage learning and knowledge retention. AlphagalorZ inspires young readers to find out more about the subjects that most interest them!

The "Guess what?" feature expands the reading and learning experience by offering additional information and fascinating facts about specific words or concepts. The "More Words" section provides additional related A to Z vocabulary words that develop and increase reading comprehension.

These books are appropriate for library, classroom, and home use.

Aa

Addition

Addition is putting numbers together into one sum.

Becky has 2 apples and 3 bananas. When she adds them all together, Becky has a total of 5 pieces of fruit (2 + 3 = 5).

Angle

An angle is made when two lines meet at the same point.

Each corner on Kyle's desk is an angle.

Billion

One billion is the numeral 1,000,000,000. It has nine zeros!

Kari will have lived a billion seconds when she is 31 years, eight months, and nine days old.

Guess what?

A stack of one billion pennies would be almost one thousand miles high!

Bb

Calculator

A calculator is a tool used to solve math problems. It can add, subtract, multiply, and divide.

Guess what?

You should use a calculator only if your teacher says it is okay.

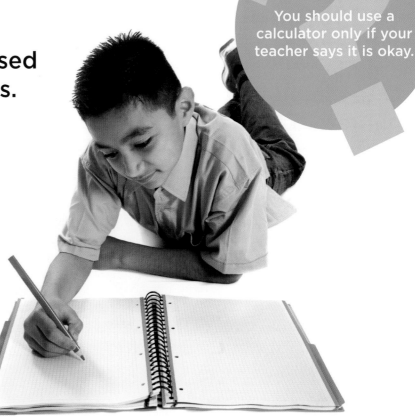

After Kevin does his math homework, he will check his answers with a calculator.

Division

Division splits a number into equal groups or parts. The ÷ sign is used in division sentences.

Melissa brought 8 pieces of candy to share with 4 friends. They will each get 2 pieces of candy (8 ÷ 4 = 2).

Dd

Diameter

A diameter is a line segment that goes through the center of a circle. It divides the circle in half.

Katie can divide a pie into two equal pieces by cutting along the diameter.

Estimate

To estimate means to find a number that is close to an exact number. You estimate when the exact number is not known or not needed.

To raise money for his school, Mike sold 4 candy bars on Monday, 6 on Tuesday, 5 on Wednesday, and 7 on Thursday. He estimates that he sold about 20 candy bars.

Ee

Even Number

An even number is a whole number that can be divided by two with nothing left over.

Liz and her friend practice their team cheer. It includes even numbers. "Two, four, six, eight, who do we appreciate? Tigers! Tigers! Go-o-o Tigers!"

Foot

One foot is the same as 12 inches. Feet and inches are used to measure length.

Last year Leah was four feet tall. She grew two inches. Now Leah is four feet and two inches tall.

Ef

Guess what?

$\frac{1}{6}$ is pronounced one-sixth.

Fraction

A fraction expresses part of a whole.

The swimming pool is divided into six lanes. If Steve wants to swim in one lane, he will take up one out of six lanes, or $\frac{1}{6}$ of the pool. The top number tells how many parts of the whole we are counting and the bottom number tells how many parts there are in the whole.

Graph

A graph is a drawing that allows us to compare numbers.

This bar graph shows that gym is the favorite subject of Mr. Hanson's class.

Gg

Guess what?

Bar, line, and picture graphs are a few of the kinds of graphs used in math.

Hundred Chart

The hundred chart can help us see patterns in numbers.

Brian sees that all of the squares below the number 1 have numbers that end in 1.

1	2	3	4	5	6	7	8	9	10
11	12	13	14	15	16	17	18	19	20
21	22	23	24	25	26	27	28	29	30
31	32	33	34	35	36	37	38	39	40
41	42	43	44	45	46	47	48	49	50
51	52	53	54	55	56	57	58	59	60
61	62	63	64	65	66	67	68	69	70
71	72	73	74	75	76	77	78	79	80
81	82	83	84	85	86	87	88	89	90
91	92	93	94	95	96	97	98	99	100

Inch

An inch is used to
measure length.
There are 12 inches
in a foot. Many rulers
are 12 inches long.

Maddy measures her pencil every
time she sharpens it. When it was
new, her pencil was seven inches
long. Now it is four inches long.

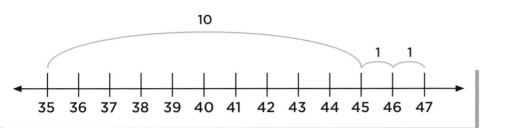

Jump Strategy

The jump strategy is a way of adding and subtracting by 10s and 1s on a number line.

When Matt adds 35 and 12, he counts 35 + 10 + 1 + 1. The sum is 47.

Kk

Kilogram

A kilogram is used to measure weight. One kilogram is equal to 1,000 grams.

Kilometer

A kilometer is used to measure distance. One kilometer is equal to 1,000 meters, which is about 3,281 feet.

Guess what?

Kilo means 1,000.

Kiloliter

A kiloliter is used to measure capacity. One kiloliter is equal to 1,000 liters.

Length

Length measures how long something is. Knowing the length of something can be very helpful.

Molly measures the length of her spoon to make sure it will fit in her lunch bag. The spoon is 5 inches long and the lunch bag is 9 inches long. Molly knows the spoon will fit!

Multiplication

Multiplication is another way to add equal groups.

Colin has 2 plates of sugar cookies. Each plate has 6 cookies. To find the total number of cookies, he multiplies 2 by 6. He has a total of 12 cookies (2 × 6 = 12).

Mm

Million

One **million** is the numeral 1,000,000. It has six zeros!

Metric System

The **metric system** is a system of measurement used in most of the world. It uses meters to measure length, liters to measure capacity, and grams to measure weight.

Numbers

Numbers are the concept we use to tell how much or how many. We can use words or numerals, such as *two* and 2, to represent numbers.

Kris is nine years old. She has three people in her family. Kris has one dog and two cats. They all live in one house.

Nn

Odd Number

An odd number is a whole number that cannot be divided evenly by two.

When Cara starts at 1 and counts every other number, she is counting the odd numbers. 1, 3, 5, 7, 9, and 11 are odd numbers.

Ordinal Number

An ordinal number tells the order or position of something. We use them to tell where or which one we mean.

Patrick can tell his friend which house is his. It is the third house from the corner. First, second, third, and fourth are ordinal numbers.

Parallel Lines

Parallel lines are lines that never intersect. They can be found in many places.

Look at the gutters next to the bowling lane. They are parallel lines. The gutters will never meet.

Qq

Quotient

A quotient is the answer to a division problem.

10 children want to play kickball. They need to make 2 teams. 10 divided by 2 equals five. There will be 5 children on each team. 5 is the quotient, or answer, to the problem (10 ÷ 2 = 5).

Remainder

A remainder is an amount left over after subtracting one number from another.

Ben has 5 hours to finish his homework and play outside with friends. It takes him 2 hours to do his homework. That leaves him 3 hours to play with friends. 3 hours is the remainder (5 − 2 = 3).

Guess what?

There are also remainders in division.

Rr

Round

Round a number up or down to estimate how many things there are. You usually round to the nearest 5 or 10.

Genny picked 47 cherries from one tree and 32 cherries from another tree. She rounds 47 up to 50 and rounds 32 down to 30. Then she can add 50 and 30 to find that she picked about 80 cherries.

Subtraction

Subtraction is taking away an amount from the total number.

Ryan has 15 soccer games during the summer. He has already played 5 games. If he subtracts 5 from 15, Ryan knows he has 10 games left (15 – 5 = 10).

Guess what?

The minus sign (–) is used in subtraction sentences.

Scale

A scale is a tool for measuring weight.

Erin wants to send a package to her friend. The cost to mail the package is based on the weight of the package. The postal clerk weighs the package on the scale to see how heavy the package is and how much it will cost to send it.

Table

A multiplication table is a chart of multiplication facts.

	1	2	3	4	5	6	7	8	9	10
1	1	2	3	4	5	6	7	8	9	10
2	2	4	6	8	10	12	14	16	18	20
3	3	6	9	12	15	18	21	24	27	30
4	4	8	12	16	20	24	28	32	36	40
5	5	10	15	20	25	30	35	40	45	50
6	6	12	18	24	30	36	42	48	54	60
7	7	14	21	28	35	42	49	56	63	70
8	8	16	24	32	40	48	56	64	72	80
9	9	18	27	36	45	54	63	72	81	90
10	10	20	30	40	50	60	70	80	90	100

Example: 3 × 7 = 21

Trillion

One trillion is the numeral 1,000,000,000,000. It has twelve zeros!

Sharon wonders how many years a trillion seconds would last. A trillion seconds would last over 31,688 years!

Ms. Sand's class uses a multiplication table to memorize multiplication facts. They find the factors they want to multiply and then follow across the row and down the column to see where they meet. That is the answer!

Uu

U.S. Currency

Each country has currency, or money, that people use to buy and sell things. The United States has its own currency. The unit of measurement is the dollar. Parts of a dollar are cents.

one dollar = 100 cents

penny
(1 cent)

nickel
(5 cents)

dime
(10 cents)

quarter
(25 cents)

Volume

Volume measures the amount of space a 3-D object takes up or holds.

Volume is measured in cubic units. To find the volume of this box, Kathy will multiply the length, width, and height. The volume of this box is 2 cubic feet. 2 × 1 × 1 = 2

width = 1 foot

length = 2 feet

height = 1 foot

Guess what?

3-D stands for three-dimensional.

Weight

Weight a measure of how heavy something is. Weight is measured in units such as kilograms and pounds. A scale is used to measure weight.

Guess what?

An ocean sunfish caught off the coast of Japan in 1996 may be the world's heaviest bony fish. It weighed 5,071 pounds!

John can measure the weight of the fish he caught.

Ww

X-axis

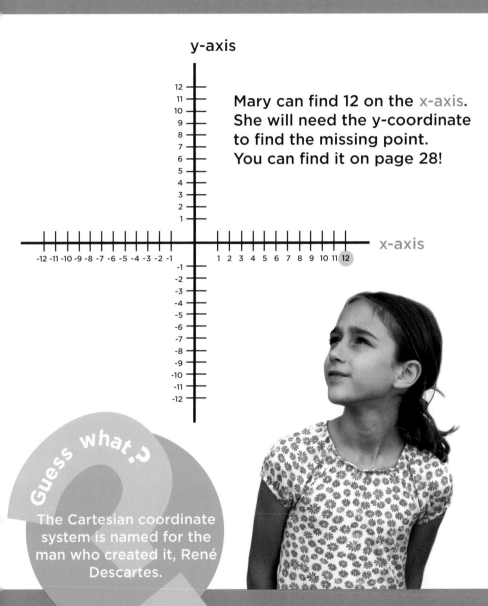

y-axis

x-axis

Mary can find 12 on the x-axis. She will need the y-coordinate to find the missing point. You can find it on page 28!

The Cartesian coordinate system uses a vertical number line and a horizontal number line to locate points. The horizontal line is called the X-axis.

You can find it on page 28!

Guess what?

The Cartesian coordinate system is named for the man who created it, René Descartes.

Y-axis

In the Cartesian coordinate system, the vertical line is called the y-axis. You need to know one point on the x-axis and one point on the y-axis to find a spot on the coordinate system.

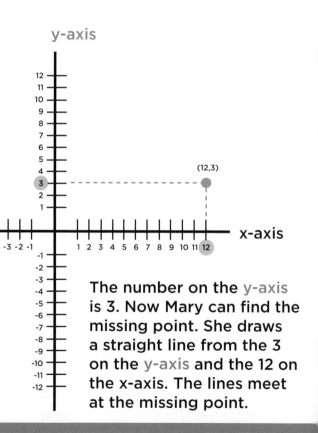

The number on the y-axis is 3. Now Mary can find the missing point. She draws a straight line from the 3 on the y-axis and the 12 on the x-axis. The lines meet at the missing point.

Zillion

A zillion isn't a real number. But it is a real word. We say *zillion* when a number is so big we can't define it!

Zz

Zero

Zero is a symbol for an amount that equals nothing. When zero is added to any number, the number remains the same.

3+0=3

Glossary

3-D – having length, width, and height and taking up space.

appreciate – to value or admire greatly.

capacity – the most that something can hold.

coordinate – one of two numbers used to locate a point on a plane.

distance – the amount of space between two places.

gutter – a groove that catches and guides things.

horizontal – in the same direction as, or parallel to, the ground.

intersect – to meet and cross at a point.

liter – a metric unit used to measure volume. One liter is equal to 33.8 ounces.

meter – a unit of measurement in the metric system. A meter is slightly longer than a yard in the U.S. customary system.

package – an item that has been wrapped or placed in a box.

strategy – a careful plan.

tool – a device that helps you do a chore.

unit – a group that contains a specific number or amount.

vertical – at a right angle, or perpendicular to, the ground.

whole number – any of the counting or natural numbers, such as 1, 2, 3, and so on. Zero is a whole number, but fractions and negative numbers are not.

More Math!

Can you learn about these math terms too?

algebra	geometry	quadrillion
bar graph	greater than	quintillion
base ten	hemisphere	radius
calendar	horizontal line	rectangle
Celsius	hundred	right angle
circle	integer	similarity
compass	intersecting lines	square
cone	mass	square number
cube	negative number	symmetry
cylinder	numerator	temperature
decimal	obtuse angle	time
degree	percent	trapezoid
denominator	perimeter	triangle
double	positive number	unit fraction
equation	prediction	unit of measurement
Fahrenheit	prism	variable
fluid ounce	probability	whole number
gallon	pyramid	yard